WALT DISNEY'S

Snow White
and the Seven Dwarfs

P9-CQD-404

Adapted by Liza Baker
Illustrated by Atelier Philippe Harchy

Once upon a time, there lived a lovely young princess named Snow White. Her stepmother, the Queen, was jealous of Snow White's beauty.

One day, Snow White was singing in the courtyard. A handsome young prince was riding by and heard her beautiful voice. He climbed the castle wall to find her. But shy Snow White ran up to her balcony.

From the courtyard below, the Prince sang to Snow White. She listened happily to his song and did not see the evil Queen watching them.

Every day, the Queen would ask, "Magic Mirror on the wall, who is the fairest one of all?"

Each time the mirror would answer, "You are."

But one day the mirror replied, "A lovely maid I see, who is more fair than thee."

"It's Snow White!" snarled the Queen.

Enraged with jealousy, the Queen ordered her huntsman to take Snow White into the forest and kill her.

The huntsman led Snow White deep into the woods, but he could not harm her. "I can't do as the Queen wishes!" he cried. "Run away, child, and never come back!"

Snow White fled into the forest. But the woods were dark and scary. She fell to the ground and began to cry.

Wiping her eyes, Snow White looked up and found herself surrounded by forest animals. "Do you know where I can stay?" she asked them.

The friendly animals led Snow White to a tiny cottage in the woods.

"It's like a doll's house!" said Snow White. She knocked at the door, but no one answered. "May I come in?" she called. Slowly, she stepped inside.

As Snow White wandered through the house, she discovered seven little chairs and seven little beds.

"Seven little children must live here! Let's clean the house and surprise them," she suggested to the woodland creatures. "Then maybe they'll let me stay."

Close by, the seven dwarfs who lived in the cottage were busy working in their mine. All day long they dug for jewels.

At five o'clock their workday was over. Doc, Grumpy, Happy, Sleepy, Sneezy, Bashful, and Dopey marched home, singing and whistling as they went.

When the dwarfs reached their cottage, the light was on—someone was in their house! They crept inside and tiptoed upstairs to find Snow White fast asleep beneath their blankets!

"It's a monster!" whispered one dwarf.

Stepping closer, Doc cried out, "Why, it's a girl!"

Snow White sat up and said, "How do you do?"

She explained to the dwarfs who she was and what the evil Queen had tried to do to her. "Don't send me away," she begged. "If you let me stay, I'll wash and sew and sweep and cook."

At that, the dwarfs shouted, "Hooray! She stays!"

Back at the castle, the Queen asked the mirror once again, "Who now is the fairest one of all?"

"Over the seven jeweled hills beyond the seventh fall, in the cottage of the seven dwarfs dwells Snow White, the fairest one of all," answered the mirror.

The angry Queen drank a potion that disguised her as an old hag. Then she created a magic apple. "After she takes one bite of this poisoned apple, Snow White's eyes will close forever," she said with a cackle. The only cure for the sleeping spell would be love's first kiss.

Unaware of the Queen's plot, Snow White and the Seven Dwarfs sang and danced late into the night.

The next morning, Snow White kissed all the dwarfs good-bye before they marched off for the mine.

Doc warned the princess, "The Queen is a sly one. Beware of strangers!"

From the shadows of the trees, the Queen watched the dwarfs leave. Slowly, she crept up to the cottage.

"All alone, my pet?" she asked Snow White. Then she offered her the poisoned apple. "Go on, dearie. Have a bite."

Several birds recognized the wicked queen and knocked the apple from her hand. But Snow White felt sorry for the old woman and helped her inside the cottage.

Sensing danger, the forest animals ran off to warn the dwarfs. But it was too late.

Snow White bit into the poisoned fruit! She dropped the apple and fell to the floor.

"Now I'll be the fairest in the land!" said the Queen with a cackle.

Lightning flashed and thunder cracked as she fled from the cottage.

But before the Queen could escape, the Seven Dwarfs returned.

"After her!" cried Grumpy.

The dwarfs chased the Queen to the top of a rocky cliff.

"I'll fix you!" she shrieked as she tried to roll an enormous boulder down on them.

Suddenly, a bolt of lightning struck the ledge where the Queen stood! The rock crumbled beneath her feet, and she tumbled down into the darkness below and disappeared forever.

The heartbroken dwarfs built a coffin for Snow White and watched over her day and night. Then one day the Prince who had first seen Snow White in the courtyard appeared.

He had been searching far and wide for the beautiful princess he had serenaded.

With great sorrow, he kissed Snow White farewell.

Slowly, Snow White began to awaken. The Prince's kiss had broken the spell!

Snow White thanked the dwarfs for all they had done. Together, she and the Prince rode off to his castle, where they lived happily ever after.